Scissors, Paper, & Sharing

by Anastasia Suen
illustrated by Jeff Ebbeler

Content Consultant:
Vicki F. Panaccione, Ph.D.
Licensed Child Psychologist
Founder, Better Parenting Institute

visit us at
www.abdopublishing.com

Printed in the United States.

Text by Anastasia Suen
Illustrations by Jeff Ebbeler
Edited by Patricia Stockland
Interior layout and design by Becky Daum
Cover design by Becky Daum

Library of Congress Cataloging-in-Publication Data
Suen, Anastasia.
  Scissors, paper, and sharing / Anastasia Suen ; illustrated by Jeffery Ebbeler.
      p. cm. — (Main Street school)
  Summary: When most of the paper and all of the scissors have been taken for the art project, Omar and Alex find a creative way to do their project.
  ISBN-13: 978-1-60270-032-1
  [1. Sharing—Fiction. 2. Art—Fiction. 3. Schools—Fiction.] I. Ebbeler, Jeffrey, ill. II. Title.
  PZ7.S94343Sc 2007
  [E]—dc22
                              2007004694

Omar and Alex walked into Mrs. Calhoun's art room. "I hope Mrs. Calhoun comes back soon," said Omar.

"Me, too," said Alex. "Miss Alice is a nice substitute, but it's not the same."

"Okay, class," said Miss Alice. "Today, we're going to make a quilt."

"Sewing!" said Alex. "Yuck!"

"We have all of this paper," said Miss Alice. "Come and grab what you want and get started."

Omar raised his hand. "A quilt isn't made from paper. It's made from cloth."

"We don't have time to sew," said Miss Alice. "Mrs. Calhoun is coming back tomorrow."

"Mrs. Calhoun is coming back!"
said the class.

"Didn't I tell you?" asked Miss Alice.

Omar look at Alex. Alex just shrugged.

"We have to get started right away," said Miss Alice. "We want this room to look wonderful!"

Omar raised his hand again.

"Yes, Omar?" asked Miss Alice.

"How are we going to make a quilt out of paper?" asked Omar.

"Didn't I tell you?" asked Miss Alice. Omar shook his head.

"Oh," said Miss Alice. "Everyone will make a square. We'll put them on the bulletin board. Then it will look like a quilt."

"Thank you," said Omar.

"Now come and get your paper," said Miss Alice. "Hurry, we don't have much time."

Suddenly, the front table was surrounded.

By the time Omar and Alex got to the paper box, there was hardly any paper left.

"Great," said Alex. "Mrs. Calhoun always passed out one sheet at a time. Then we had enough for everyone."

"No one would act like this if Mrs. Calhoun were here," said Omar. "Poor Miss Alice just doesn't know the rules."

"What can I make with brown and yellow paper?" said Alex.

Omar pointed at the poster behind Mrs. Calhoun's desk. "That poster only has two colors," said Omar.

"But that poster isn't a quilt," said Alex.

"True," said Omar. "But this is all we have."

Alex walked to the other end of the table. "There aren't any scissors left either!"

"It's a good thing Mrs. Calhoun is coming back tomorrow," said Omar.

"But what will we do today?" asked Alex.

Omar took his paper and tore it in half. *Rip!* "We'll cut it like this!"

Alex laughed.

"You crack me up, Omar," said Alex.

"A Cub Scout is always prepared," said Omar.

"Okay," said Alex. "What do we do next?"

"We tear the paper," said Omar.

"Really?" asked Alex.

"Really," said Omar. "That's what we did when Mrs. Calhoun was here."

"We did?" asked Alex.

"We did when we made those mosaics," said Omar.

"I remember that," said Alex. "Let's do it."

Omar and Alex tore their paper into little squares.

"What are you guys doing?" asked Dalton.

"Making a mosaic," said Alex.

"Can I do it, too?" asked Dalton.

"Sure," said Omar. "Come sit with us so we can share paper."

"Good idea," said Dalton. He moved his chair over to Omar's table.

"I'll tear this red paper," said Dalton.

"Here are some brown squares," said Omar.

"I'm almost done with the yellow," said Alex.

"We need a paper to glue the squares on,"
said Omar. He walked back to the table.
There were three small sheets of paper left.

"So far, so good," said Alex.

"Now what?" asked Dalton.

"We make a pattern with the squares,"
said Omar.

Omar put a brown square in the corner.
Then he added another brown square and
a red square.

"We have a lot of brown," said Omar.
He added two more brown squares.

"This is like math," said Alex. "It's two, one,
and two."

"Don't forget the yellow squares,"
said Dalton.

"Something's missing," said Alex.

"Glue," said Omar.

Alex looked at the supply table. "There isn't any glue left," said Alex.

"I have some glue," said Dalton. "We can share it."

"Thanks," said Omar. "Sharing is the only way we can get this done."

What Do You Think?

1. What happened when Miss Alice didn't
    share enough information about
    the project?

2. Why do you think Mrs. Calhoun always
    passed out one sheet of paper at
    a time?

3. What did the boys have to do when the
    art supplies ran out?

Words to Know

mosaic—a pattern or picture made up of small pieces.
prepare—to make or get ready.
quilt—a warm, usually padded, cover for a bed.
share—to divide something between two or more people.
substitute—something or someone used in place of another.

Miss K's Classroom Rules

1.   Take only what you need.
2.   Work with others to get things done.
3.   Let others use what you have, too.
4.   Give away things you don't need anymore.

Web Sites

To learn more about sharing, visit ABDO Publishing Company on the World Wide Web at **www.abdopublishing.com**. Web sites about sharing are featured on our Book Links page. These links are routinely monitored and updated to provide the most current information available.